The House
in the Tree

The House
in the Tree

Bianca Pitzorno

Illustrated by
Quentin Blake

Translated by
Stephen Parkin

ALMA BOOKS

ALMA BOOKS LTD
3 Castle Yard
Richmond
Surrey TW10 6TF
United Kingdom
www.almabooks.com

The House in the Tree first published in Italian 1999 as *La casa sull'albero*
This translation first published by Alma Books Ltd in 2017

Text © Arnoldo Mondadori Editori S.p.A., Milano, 1999
Text © Mondadori Libri S.p.A., Milano, 2015
Translation © Stephen Parkin, 2017
Illustrations and cover image © Quentin Blake

Printed in Great Britain by CPI Group (UK) Ltd, Croydon CR0 4YY

ISBN: 978-1-84688-410-8

Contents

A Really Unusual Tree   3

A Curious Neighbour   9

Problems with the Neighbours   16

A Feat of Hydraulic Engineering   21

The Migration Season   27

A Present from the Storks   36

A Party in the Tree   41

The Tenant's Curse   50

The Children Change Diet   55

Infant Lispings   63

The Intoxication of Flight   72

Signals in the Night   80

The Great Battle   88

Afterword   96

For Aglaia,
who exists for real —
as does Bianca,
who is none other
than the Author

A Really Unusual Tree

When you first saw it, it seemed a tree just like any other tree. It stood in the middle of a field on a gentle slope. Its trunk was quite thick, and it was covered with dense foliage.

The bark of the trunk was brown, and wrinkled knotty roots spread out around its base.

The leaves were green and thick, but they were too high up for you to see their shapes properly. At the foot of the tree there were clumps of grass, daisies, little stones and, whenever it rained, a few red-capped mushrooms, just like the ones you see in the pictures of a book. There were flowers and fruits on the branches, and butterflies, bees and little birds among them... It was just like any other tree.

But if you looked closely, you could see, at the bottom of the tree, a little door hidden among the knotty roots. It was wide enough to enter without getting stuck (unless you were a bit too fat). The trunk was in fact hollow, and inside it a little spiral staircase ran all the way up to the branches and the leaves. And if you didn't want to use the secret little door, there were also broken-off branches sticking out of the trunk which went all the way up and which you could grab or step onto to climb above.

Aglaia of course preferred this way. She'd scamper up as quick as a squirrel.

She was eight years old and lived in the tree with her friend Bianca. Bianca was a grown-up. The two of them had both got tired of living in the city, in an ordinary house. So they decided to join forces: they went to look for a suitable tree and, once they'd found one, moved in.

At the top of the trunk, where the branches divided, there was a platform made from planks and surrounded by a parapet. You couldn't see it from the ground, because the leaves were so thick. In the middle of the platform there was a trapdoor through which you could run a rope down to pull anything up into the tree – a basket of food, or a piano, if you wanted one.

To get higher up, there weren't any more stairs: you had to climb from branch to branch. The tree was so tall it never seemed to stop. If you stood in the field and looked at it, it just seemed an ordinary tree – tall but not very tall. At a certain point there were no more branches, but only the sky above them.

But if you climbed up inside the tree, you wouldn't believe it – you went on climbing, up and up until you

4

felt giddy if you looked down at the field far below. But Bianca and Aglaia had never reached the top.

They had decided to build their house on a couple of sturdy branches, just a few feet above the platform. They'd worked all summer building it, busy with saws and hammers.

And they'd built a really beautiful house. It was very large, though you'd never have guessed it was there looking up from the field. It didn't have a proper plan, in the sense that the arrangement of the rooms was permanent. Only the floor and part of the roof were fixed in place. There were walls and canopies made out of leaves woven together, and you could move them about as you wanted to – depending on the sun, the wind, the heat, on whether the two of them wanted to be together or on their own, or if they needed to check what was on the horizon…

Normally, whenever the weather was fine, they rolled up the walls and put them in a corner, and the house was open on all sides.

They had all the furniture they needed: not too much, not too little. And the same was true for the other things they needed. On the other hand, there was a huge number of games and books, and whenever they ran out of space to keep them, Aglaia would tie them with string onto nearby branches.

Her bed too hung from a branch just outside the house. It was a kind of Eskimo cradle; it looked a bit like a silkworm's cocoon, or one of those bird's nests that are enclosed and woven tight. It was lined with fur and swayed to and fro whenever there was a breeze.

Bianca, however, was worried about getting rheumatism – and also suffered from seasickness – so she slept in a sleeping bag inside the tree trunk, in a little recess near the spiral staircase. "I feel safer sleeping near the door," she would say. "If a fire broke out, I could let the firemen know immediately. And if thieves tried to break in, I could stop them."

But, you must be wondering, if neither of them slept in the house, what did they use the house for?

They used it to welcome their friends who came to visit, to hold big parties, to put on plays, to do the housework and to cook. They had a beautiful kitchen, full of pots and pans, made of metal and earthenware.

Then there was a music room with all the instruments of an orchestra; a studio for painting, with coloured paints and pencils and huge sheets of paper; there was even a greenhouse. A greenhouse in a tree? Yes, that's right, a greenhouse! Actually, it was more than a greenhouse: it was a laboratory for botanical experiments. Bianca had had the idea of making their tree contain all the kinds of fruit trees that existed. Up

and down the branches she would go the whole day long making grafts. Everywhere you could see those funny-looking bandages wrapped round the branches that had been cut into, where little twigs from different types of trees had been inserted. At first all their friends laughed and said it was a crazy idea, but when Bianca started to achieve her first results they stopped criticizing.

The tree was an oak tree, so it produced acorns. But with the first grafting, one of its main branches became a walnut tree – and so, when the autumn came, Aglaia could pick fresh walnuts by leaning out of her window. Then on another branch a chestnut tree had been grafted. Higher up, Bianca had grown apple and pear and apricot trees. There was also a small cherry tree, as well as one bearing plums and another one peaches. Aglaia had begged Bianca to graft a mulberry tree, even just a small branch, and this had succeeded as well.

Then Bianca decided she'd undertake a more difficult task. Up until then she had only grafted fruit trees that were native to the place where they lived. Now she wanted to try and grow tropical plants. And after a few attempts, she succeeded in growing dates and bananas and coconuts, and then mangos and papayas, pineapples and even breadfruit.

Now they had everything, and they no longer needed to shop in a supermarket.

The best thing was that the fruit ripened in different seasons. So, at every time of the year, some branches were in blossom and some bare, others just coming into leaf and bud, while others were laden with fruit of all different colours...

"What a beautiful tree," sighed Aglaia as she stared up at it. But no one knew that she lived in a house in its branches. This was a secret shared between her, Bianca and Mr Beccaris Brullo.

A Curious Neighbour

Mr Beccaris Brullo was a difficult neighbour – or shall we say a difficult fellow resident? For he too lived in the tree, and perhaps had been living there before Bianca and Aglaia arrived. But no one knew this for certain.

At first the tree had seemed completely uninhabited. There was no sign of a name on the small secret door, and nothing on the trapdoor on the lowermost platform. There was no trace of a house on the branches the two friends had first explored, apart from the birds' nests.

So they went ahead and built their house, convinced that they were the only two occupants of the oak tree. They'd been living there two or three months when Prunilde, Bianca's black cat, had gone hunting for birds one day (they'd never managed to train her to be a vegetarian) and had climbed up onto a branch they'd never explored before.

Of course, as often happens to very young cats, she found she couldn't get down again and started to miaow for help.

Bianca was not at home, so Aglaia had to climb up to rescue her. She climbed up very nimbly, though she was a bit annoyed, as she had a lot to do in the house rather than waste time going after adventurous cats.

But when she climbed onto the unknown branch, she saw a rope with lots of knots tied in it dangling down. She looked up, but the leaves were so thick she couldn't see where the top of the rope was tied.

So, pushing Prunilde down inside her jumper, while giving her a telling-off and warning her to hold tight and not scratch, she started to climb up the rope.

She climbed and climbed, using the knots like steps, and came to a place where the main trunk divided off once more. Here there was a second platform, surrounded by a parapet of thorny branches, and in the middle of the platform there was an odd-looking shack of a house, tall and narrow like a sentry box, and all closed-up, with only a tiny door with three chains across it and an even tinier window protected by bars.

Well, whoever lived in that house didn't have much time for strangers. Instead of the usual "WELCOME", the doormat had "PUSH OFF" written on it. The barrel of a shotgun was sticking out of the window

bars, and next to the bell there was a sign which threatened:

FIERCE DOG
KEEP AWAY!
(WHILE YOU CAN)

"A dog in a tree?" Aglaia wondered. "How on earth could it have climbed up here?"

Prunilde let out a frightened "Miaow!" and dug her claws into Aglaia's shoulder. Aglaia gave her a little smack on the head to stop her.

There was no sign of life from inside the barricaded house. No sounds, no smell of cooking, no sign of movement, no lights… But there was certainly someone at home. Aglaia had the distinct feeling that someone was spying on her from somewhere, and not in a very kindly way. The thought of that gaze gave her goose pimples.

Then she lost patience. Whoever it was, how dare this stranger take up residence on their tree and – to make things worse – stare at her in that fashion?

"I couldn't care less for your rifle and your chains!" she shouted as loud as she could, and kicked the barred door. "Go on, come out of there, if you dare! What are you doing in our tree?"

"Just listen to her!" a harsh voice from inside the house grated. "Your tree? What are *you* doing in my oak?"

The door banged open, and an old man appeared on the threshold. He was dressed in dark-grey clothes and was holding a catapult.

Aglaia clenched her fists at him. "The tree is ours, so do us the favour of packing your bags and moving out!"

"Oh, so it's yours, is it? I've been watching you two come and go for quite a while now, and I've been wondering just how far your impertinence would take you. Well, just you listen to this, sweetheart: I've been living on this tree for a hundred years and more, and I don't like intruders in my neck of the woods!"

"What rubbish! A hundred years! Liar, liar – pants on fire!" replied Aglaia. "You're not even eighty... And in any case I know perfectly well you got here after we did. When we climbed the tree for the first time, there was no one living here."

"Little liar! You didn't bother to check whether there was someone else living here. You just barged your way in! You're illegal squatters, that's what you are! Push off out of here! Pack your bags and clear off! The tree's mine!"

"No it isn't, it's ours!"

"It's mine!"

It could have gone on like this for ever, but Aglaia lost patience and grabbed the old man by his beard and gave him a fierce shake. He lost his balance and fell off the branch – but Aglaia was holding tight on to his beard and managed to pull him up, teasing him that he couldn't even stand on his own two feet.

Then the old man tried to poke his fingers in her eyes, while at the same time giving her a kick in the shins. Aglaia took him by the waist and threw him down onto the floor of the platform. They rolled about hitting out at each other, like the fistfights you see in cowboy films, while blows from both of them rained down on Prunilde, who was still stuck under Aglaia's jumper and miaowed for all she was worth as she tried to get out.

Of course, at a certain point, the two rolled to the edge of the platform and fell off. They tumbled down from branch to branch (while Prunilde clung on to Aglaia, her claws embedded in her jumper) and landed on the veranda of the two friends' house, where Bianca was trying to teach an unknown dog how to play the flute.

There was a bowl of soup in front of the dog and a napkin tied around his neck. Every time he played two notes in tune on the flute, Bianca fed him a spoonful of

the soup. The sounds coming out of the flute weren't very beautiful, obviously, but for a complete beginner he was making great strides.

"Miaow," Prunilde wailed as she shot out of Aglaia's jumper quick as a flash onto a branch higher up.

Aglaia and the old man, still locked together, rolled towards the bowl of soup and upended it. The soup went all over the floor. The dog started to bark angrily. Bianca stood up, her arms akimbo. "What a way to behave!" she said. "You've made the poor creature play all wrong. Those notes weren't in the score."

But the old man, dripping soup from head to foot, pushed Aglaia away from him and moved threateningly towards the dog. "You wretched creature!" he shouted. "So this is how you guard my house! This is how you keep out intruders! You sold yourself for a bowl of soup. Traitor!"

"Ah, so you're his owner, are you? And a fine one, at that!" Bianca exclaimed as she held on to the old man's collar and lifted him off the ground. "I think I'm going to report you to the animal-protection authorities for ill treatment and malnutrition."

The old man was kicking out wildly in an attempt to hit Bianca, so she hung him by his jacket on a branch and started her interrogation. It emerged that the poor dog, starving of hunger, had shown up in the kitchen at midday to beg for some food. Bianca had seized the opportunity, while he was eating, to teach him how to play the flute: after all, Prunilde had never shown any inclination to learn – cats are just too independent-minded.

So this was the famous "fierce dog" threatened on the sign. His master starved him of food, thinking hunger would make him devour any intruder. Instead, the dog now leapt onto him, its mouth wide open.

"Help!" shrieked the old man, waving his legs in the air, suddenly crestfallen. But the dog just licked him with his huge tongue – a few big licks and all the soup spilt over him was gone.

To calm everyone down, Bianca asked the ill-tempered old man if he'd like to have a cup of tea with them – and so, seated round the table laden with biscuits, they tried to make peace. Aglaia saw that Prunilde, perched on the branch above, kept giving the dog worried looks, not daring to come any nearer.

"I'm not going to climb up and rescue you a second time!" she said to her. "You can come down. The dog's a sweetie and won't hurt you."

The dog was called Amedeo, and was indeed very good-natured. When Prunilde came down from the branch and prudently took refuge in Bianca's arms, Amedeo sniffed her from head to tail, gave her a friendly lick and went back to sit next to the flute.

"You see? What did I tell you?" said Aglaia. "The owner is more fierce than his dog. But we'll tame him as well – just wait and see."

Problems with the Neighbours

Wouldn't it be nice if we could say that from then on Bianca and Aglaia made their peace with the fierce old man? Unfortunately it didn't turn out like that.

The old man – who, as we have seen, was called Beccaris Brullo, or B.B. to friends and allies – insisted he'd always lived in the tree. There was no way of proving whether he was telling the truth or not.

"In any case, it doesn't matter," Bianca concluded. "He's such a liar that even if he admitted he arrived after us you couldn't be sure he wasn't lying about that as well."

So, since neither party was prepared to move out of the tree, they agreed on a way of living together – or rather they drew up a contract of shared tenancy. They promised not to cause any nuisance to each other, to share any repairs resulting from damage to the tree and to make no noise after eleven in the evening. Then Mr B.B. put the leash on his dog and returned home, much to the satisfaction of Prunilde, who'd been worrying all this time that she might have to share the affections of Bianca and Aglaia with that intruder Amedeo.

From that day on, their relations were not too bad, though not particularly cordial. Every now and then, Mr Beccaris Brullo would fire his gun at the roof of Aglaia's house and then say he'd missed his target. And every so often, Aglaia would throw the rubbish onto the upper platform and then claim it was a mistake, or she'd tread on his toes or pull his beard.

On occasion they came to blows, but neither of them ever ended up in hospital. Bianca kept out of the quarrel, though she did once give Mr Beccaris Brullo a birthday cake with a laxative filling. But Mr Beccaris Brullo was so mean and tight-fisted – so tight with everything – that he was also constipated as a result, and the laxative didn't cause him the slightest problem. On the contrary, he really enjoyed the cake and kept asking Bianca to bake him another one.

The old man's rudeness was extremely trying. He expected others to treat him with respect without doing the slightest thing to deserve it. And as a fellow resident he was useless. To start with, he complained all the time about Bianca's graftings, of which she was so proud.

"What are those thingumabobs?" he would moan. "I've always detested mixing up styles. An oak is a noble tree. Its leaves were used to crown heroes and poets. And this idiot goes and spoils everything with papayas. Papayas, I ask you!" Yet, he was the first to pick lots of fruit as soon as he saw it was ripe.

He also complained because he hadn't been consulted.

"As a fellow resident I have a right to have my say in deciding every innovation or improvement," he kept repeating.

But in this case, in his view, the graftings only made things worse, so if they had asked him for his opinion, he would never have approved the idea in the first place.

Bianca let him go on moaning and continued with her experiments, until one day, fed up with his complaints, she grafted a carnivorous plant onto a branch near the old man's house.

You can just imagine Mr Beccaris Brullo's terror when, on leaving his house and fussing about, making sure all the locks and bolts were secure, he suddenly felt a bite on his arm, though there was no one else on the platform!

"I must be imagining things," he said to himself, and went back to fiddling with the door. The plant immediately stretched out a tendril and bit him on the ear.

"Help, help!" the terrified old man shrieked as he jolted back. "There's an invisible enemy about! Attack him!"

The faithful Amedeo came bounding up, baying; he'd learnt to move about the tree as nimbly as a squirrel. He was a quick-witted dog, and he immediately grasped what was going on. He put himself between his master and the carnivorous plant and began to bark menacingly. At this, Beccaris Brullo realized he wasn't in any danger as long as he steered clear of the plant, and started to comb his very long beard in an attempt to appear composed.

Over the next few days, he thought long and hard about what to do. To ask Bianca for help was out of the question – he didn't want to give her the satisfaction of knowing he'd been frightened. Approaching the plant to cut it down was unthinkable. He thought of using some herbicidal spray on it, but he was scared of poisoning the whole tree and finding himself without anywhere to live.

He finally decided to try to tame the plant, just as you would with a wild animal. Despite his meanness, he took to bringing it a fillet of steak to eat every day, and since the plant was deep down quite good-natured, they soon became friends.

In any case, she'd only bitten him playfully. She'd never intended to eat him. She might be a carnivorous plant, but she certainly wasn't into human flesh! If she'd been on her own, she would have got by with flies and other insects – but seeing that Beccaris Brullo was around, she grew accustomed to eating beefsteak on a daily basis and was soon robust and flourishing.

The old man began to treat the plant like a pet which needed looking after; he even gave her a name. Isn't it funny that people don't normally give their plants names as they do with pets? Is it because pets eat or because they respond when you call them? But I've never seen a goldfish respond when called – and yet Aglaia's had a name: Sing Sing. The plant both ate and responded by waving its branches, and Beccaris Brullo decided to call her Nina.

He grew so fond of her that Amedeo was sick with jealousy. One night the poor neglected beast gathered his few belongings together – an old gnawed leash, a rubber bone, a punctured ball – and went to ask Bianca and Aglaia if they would take him in.

The following day, it took an eternity to calm down Mr Beccaris Brullo, but in the end he had to accept the sad truth: the dog preferred to live with his fellow residents. And after all, that was what the old man wanted too: Nina, the carnivorous plant, his very own Nina, was much more suitable company for him.

There was someone, however, who was decidedly unhappy with this new arrangement: Prunilde the cat. But who cares what a cat thinks when she spends most of her time just going about her own business?

A Feat of Hydraulic Engineering

One problem the residents of the tree had to deal with from the outset was the lack of running water.

A stream ran across the field; its source could be found a bit further on. But people are never happy with what they've got; Bianca and Aglaia spent sleepless nights moping about how they couldn't get water from a tap in their house.

They'd tried to build a system of hanging pipes, but the water just refused to flow upwards without the help of a pump to push it – and neither of them knew how to build a pump.

Then, one day, Bianca said: "I've got an idea! I'll build a big tank and attach it to the highest branch."

"How will you know it's the highest branch?" asked Aglaia. "We've never been as far as the top."

"I'll just tie it to a branch that is much higher up than our house. Even higher than Mr Beccaris Brullo's house."

And that's what she did. Then the two friends beavered away at it, climbing up and down the trunk with buckets and cans that they filled with water from the stream.

But when the tank was finally brimming with water, Aglaia gasped and said: "Rats! You've forgotten to fix a tap on the bottom so the water flows down to the house."

So Bianca took a drill and started to make a hole in the tank from the outside – but the tank broke into a thousand pieces and all the water poured onto the house of Mr Beccaris Brullo, turning everything upside down and blowing his portable radio, on which he liked to listen to the love songs of his youth.

In fact, he had a lot of electrical appliances, and in order to make them work he'd once carried out a theft at the local aquarium.

Of course, there was no electricity in the tree. But the old man recalled that he'd once read in an encyclopedia about a fish called an electric ray which can give an electric shock, so one moonless night he'd gone to the aquarium and had stolen a large specimen.

He kept it in a bathtub, and whenever he needed some electricity he would starve it and then make it bite the plug of the appliance he wished to use. I know it's hard to believe – but the electric ray was so keen that all Mr Beccaris Brullo's domestic appliances just whirred along beautifully, without a hitch.

On that particular day, the water cascading down from the tank blew the valves in the radio. For the first time in its life, it was the ray who got an electric shock.

Beccaris Brullo was furious and called an extraordinary residents' meeting in which he berated the two friends. "I forbid the two of you from carrying out any more criminal experiments!" he shouted at them.

"But what are you getting so angry about?" said Bianca, trying to calm him down. "If we succeed in getting some plumbing installed, you too will get the benefit of it. You'll be able to add another electrical appliance to your collection: a boiler."

But all such efforts proved futile.

As time went by, so the need to have running water in the house increased. Bianca and Aglaia spent their days scratching themselves as if they had nits – even though they bathed in the stream three times a day.

It was just the thought they didn't have a bathtub which made them feel unwashed.

In the end, out of desperation, they decided to kidnap the plumber who did work for Aglaia's grandmother, a certain Mr Ceglie.

You might be thinking: wouldn't it have been easier just to ask him if he'd come and take a look at the pipes? Oh yes, of course – and then he would discover where the tree was and he would tell everyone about it, when it was supposed to be a secret.

So one night they tiptoed into his house, trussed him up like a salami while he was sleeping, put a blindfold over his eyes and carried him as far as the foot of the tree. They pushed him – still fast asleep – through the little door, hauled him up the stairs as far as the platform and then applied ice packs to wake him up, though they didn't take the blindfold off his eyes.

"Where am I? What's happened to my legs and my arms? Why can't I move them?" Mr Ceglie exclaimed as he woke up and found himself all tied up like a parcel.

"You're in New York, at the top of the Statue of Liberty. Now climb!" Bianca said in a nasty voice while poking his ribs with an umbrella. She hoped he might think it was a gun, given he couldn't see anything.

"Oh what a horrible dream I'm having!" he said, annoyed. "It must be that cabbage I ate last night. I must remember to tell the wife not to give me cabbage any more."

"Cut the cackle and do as you're told!" Aglaia curtly interrupted.

They pushed him up the stairs, still prodding him with the umbrella, and when they were inside the house they carried him into the room they planned to turn into the bathroom and said: "Now fix us a basin and a tub with two taps each. And then a toilet with a chain, and a bidet – and, since you're at it, a shower as well."

"How on earth can I work if you don't take the blindfold off my eyes?" wailed their prisoner. "What stupid people you meet in dreams!"

"And so we're crazy enough to take the blindfold off to let you go and blab to everyone about what you've seen?"

"Don't worry, I never remember anything I dream about, ever. You can be sure of that."

"You think you're dreaming – but, oh boy, are you mistaken! Quit wasting time and do what I tell you!" Aglaia replied.

"But how can I install plumbing if I can't see anything?" poor Mr Ceglie protested.

"Just work it out!" Aglaia said menacingly, digging the umbrella into his side.

And so Mr Ceglie, groping in the dark, did all the jobs they'd ordered him to do, though the taps were crooked and the water squirted in every direction except the correct one. So when they washed, they had to

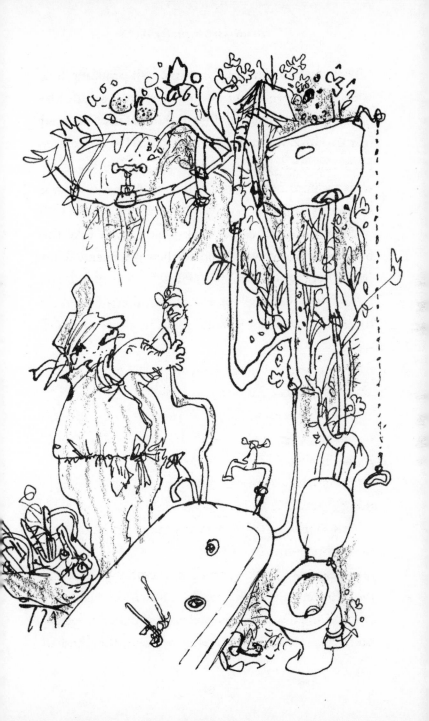

put themselves in the oddest positions, hanging on to the branches high up or dangling sideways out of the window or from the platform. But that didn't matter: the two friends were extremely pleased to have running water in the house.

They gave Mr Ceglie, still wearing his blindfold, something to eat and drink and then carried him back to bed.

He woke up the next morning full of aches and pains and complained to his wife: "Oh, what a terrible dream. Never cook cabbage for dinner again!"

The Migration Season

Shortly after this, there was the episode of the storks, which certainly didn't make the residents' life in the tree any easier. On the contrary!

This is what happened. Over several weeks Aglaia had noticed that every evening towards sunset a flock of storks flew over the tree on their way south. Not the same flock of storks, of course! Each evening there was a new one.

"It must be the time of year they migrate," thought Aglaia. "My teacher in school told me how in winter these birds move to countries with milder climates, because they don't like the cold. But I think they also get fed up with being always in the same place. They get itchy feet, just like swallows."

But swallows are small birds – though they are very elegant – and they can't carry heavy weights. And things might have turned out a lot better if the birds had been swallows rather than storks.

Mr Beccaris Brullo has also seen the storks on several occasions. In fact, each evening, when they flew over, he would station himself at his window looking at the sky through a spyglass. "He must like birds," Aglaia thought. "Perhaps he's a naturalist. Perhaps he's writing a book on storks."

On the contrary: Mr Beccaris Brullo was planning a terrible revenge. His neighbours had failed to notice that one of the storks in the first flock, flying directly over the tree, had done a number two on Mr B.B.'s roof.

The tiles of Mr B.B.'s roof were so clean they gleamed. He spent all his time rubbing and polishing them, using all the latest cleaning products recommended on the telly (yes, Mr Beccaris Brullo also had a television, and the poor electric ray had to work flat out to keep it going).

Mr B.B. had covered the roof tiles with a transparent varnish to protect them from the weather. Whenever it rained, he opened a huge umbrella over the house in order to protect the roof from the rain.

But he also worried about the umbrella. He thought of building a second roof to protect the umbrella which was protecting the first roof... He asked Bianca for advice, and she suggested he did nothing. After all, he could put the umbrella into the washing machine whenever it got dirty, and it would come out as good as new, or even better.

But on the day the stork pooed on Mr Beccaris Brullo's roof, the weather was perfect and the roof was unprotected and open to the skies.

One of the storks – who knows if she did it just because she was mischievous or because she had the runs and couldn't hold out till she reached the next toilet? – had done a bright-yellow poo right on the immaculate tiles, which had splashed everywhere, just like pigeons' droppings.

But this had happened days before. The roof had been thoroughly recleaned, and anyone would have expected Mr Beccaris Brullo to have forgotten about the incident completely. Not a bit of it! He wanted revenge, so he waited at the window with his spyglass and a shotgun ready to take aim as soon as a stork flew low enough to be within range.

At last, one Sunday afternoon, a small group of storks – the last stragglers, since by now the weather had turned cold – emerged from behind the hill and headed towards the tree.

Aglaia was outside, putting a tray of biscuits she'd just taken out of the oven on the branch so they could cool down.

Perhaps those biscuits were to blame for the storks coming to a sticky end, or perhaps it was destiny.

Anyway, the flock started to descend, almost as if they were heading for Aglaia's branch.

At the same moment Mr Beccaris Brullo seized hold of his shotgun.

"Stop, you idiot! What do you think you're doing?" Bianca screamed at him.

It was a pointless question, since it was perfectly obvious what he was up to. *Bang-bang-bang!* Three shots up in the air and three storks fell onto the tree, while the rest of the flock hurried on their way eastwards squawking loudly and flapping their wings in indignation.

A satisfied Mr B.B. closed the shutters, completely uninterested in what became of the three birds which had fallen from the sky.

But Aglaia rushed up to the top of the tree, climbing swiftly through the branches, led by the groans of the three storks, who had each fallen on branches at different heights. By good luck, none of them had been seriously hurt. The shot from Mr Beccaris Brullo's gun wasn't large enough to really hurt someone.

The oldest stork had lost five feathers from its wings and couldn't fly straight.

The second stork had grazed its knee. Storks have very long legs, so their knees are very high up.

The third stork had twisted its neck. Storks have very long necks, and when their necks hurt they hurt a lot, because there's so much neck hurting. Just like giraffes.

When she realized the storks hadn't been seriously hurt, Aglaia started to scold them.

"Oh, stop your whining, for Heaven's sake!" she exclaimed. "I don't see why you don't fly on with the others. You can't fly in a straight line? Well, put up with it! All you need to do is hold on to the legs of the stork in front of you."

But the storks finally confessed that in reality they'd taken advantage of the incident because they were tired of following the flock.

"We like to think for ourselves, you see! In the first place, we were tired and needed a rest. And then the smell of your biscuits… That's what decided us to stop for a bit at your place."

"Excuse me," replied Aglaia. "I made the biscuits for a friend of mine whose birthday it is tomorrow. So I'll thank you for not touching them! As for needing to rest, you'll have to ask Mr B.B. We share this tree with him, so we need to hear what he thinks."

While talking to the three storks, she'd noticed that each was carrying a large bundle tied to its beak.

"That must be their baggage," she thought. "You need to pack a lot for a long journey. You think they'd have bought themselves some suitcases."

Just at that moment Bianca arrived, accompanied by Prunilde the cat.

As soon as the storks saw the cat, they started to flap their wings and screech. Prunilde was just about to pounce, but then thought better of it: there were three of them, and they were a lot larger than she was. So she started licking a paw with an air of total indifference, while remaining close to Bianca's legs. But she could hardly contain her curiosity at the sight of the bundles; her whiskers quivered with excitement.

Bianca took one look at the three storks and shook her head.

"What've you got in those bundles?" she asked accusingly. She knew perfectly well what they had, but she wanted to get the storks to admit it.

"Babies, of course," the storks replied, as if it was the most obvious thing in the world.

"Oh, don't make me laugh! No one's silly enough to believe any more that storks go around carrying babies!" exclaimed Aglaia. "Everyone knows you need mothers to make babies…"

"Is that so? Well, it's news to us," replied the storks with an offended air. "No one ever bothered to inform us."

"That's all very well, but just where are you taking these babies?" Bianca asked severely.

"To three families who've ordered them," the storks replied. "Obviously nobody had told them either that we don't carry babies."

"So, instead of making their own," the second stork added, "they sent us a postcard by airmail and a form for payment on receipt of goods."

"We're known for our motto," said the third. "Try them out free for a week and get your money back if you're not satisfied. Haven't you ever heard of mail order?"

"Just listen to their fibs," Bianca said to Aglaia. "What is the world coming to? The kind of people you come across nowadays…"

"Storks are people?" asked Aglaia.

"If they're in a story they are," replied Bianca. Then she turned to the storks. "OK, show us these babies, then!"

"I rather fear mine will have got bumped about a bit when we landed on the tree," said the first stork. "If you like, I can offer you a discount on the listed price…"

"Mine too won't be in tip-top condition after our accident," the other stork added. "I rather expect the clients will want to return the order. If you on the other hand would like to take it, I'm sure we could strike a good deal."

"That's all we need – second-hand babies!" Bianca exclaimed in despair. "We already have to put up with Mr B.B."

But the storks had unwrapped their bundles and were proudly displaying their merchandise.

"Just look at this marvel!" exclaimed the first. "A chubby little boy, four kilos, red hair and all his fingers and toes in the right place! He's yours for eighty-three biscuits and two kilos of quinces…"

The second was also singing the praises of its baby: a little black girl with a thick shock of hair almost falling onto her shoulders.

The third stork meanwhile had very carefully unwrapped its bundle to reveal the showpiece of the three samples: a pair of twins, one boy and one girl, both tiny, in dirty nappies and bawling their heads off. Typical newborn babies.

"Hmm, 'newborn'," thought Aglaia. "But if they've not yet been delivered to the families who ordered them, can they really be described as born, or not?"

"It's a real bargain" the storks repeated. "If you take all four, we can reduce the price even further. Buy two, get four!"

"Wrap them up again and take them away!" Bianca retorted angrily. "We haven't ordered them. We don't buy from street traders or travelling salesmen. Take yourselves off!"

The storks were abashed at Bianca's determined tone and started to wrap the babies up again. They hooked the bundles to their beaks, lifted themselves on their long legs and started to stretch their wings, ready to fly away.

"And about time too!" thought Prunilde. "Bunch of time-wasters." She had followed the conversation with much anxiety. Now, with an air of satisfaction, she arched her back and directed a contemptuous miaow at the three birds.

A Present from the Storks

As the storks were pointing their beaks to the south and opening their wings for take-off, a doubt struck Aglaia.

"Where will you take the babies, seeing we don't want them?" she asked.

"To the families who ordered them in the first place," replied the first stork. "That's if they still want them, of course... We've lost so much time because you shot at us that I dare say they've made other arrangements by now."

"And if they don't want them?"

"We'll take them back to the warehouse until a new order is placed."

"Oh!"

"But," the second stork added, "who knows if there will be a new order? Now everyone knows you make babies at home and the storks don't bring them. Who knows if we'll find three families stupid enough to write to us..."

So... could they leave four babies in the care of such ignorant and irresponsible birds? Of course not. Bianca started to shout and clap her hands: "Just leave the bundles on the branch, you wretches, and fly off! Shoo, shoo! We won't give you a penny for this runny-nosed shop-soiled lot. Just think yourselves lucky we're not going to ask you for a warranty."

"Yes, that's right! Shoo! Or I'll get the gun and shoot at you again!" Aglaia added.

As soon as the gun was mentioned, the storks forgot all their aches and pains and dumped the bundles so unceremoniously that one of them rolled off onto a branch below. Then, flapping their wings noisily, they flew away.

But they really were the most provoking creatures. One of them snatched three biscuits from the tray, while another pooed all over Mr Beccaris Brullo's immaculate roof. Again!

"And now we've got three – or rather four – babies to look after," sighed Bianca, while Aglaia went to fetch the one which had fallen on the branch below.

"We could try giving them to Mr B.B." Aglaia suggested a bit later. "After all, he was the one who shot at the storks. If they hadn't fallen into our tree, the babies would now be with their families."

"I suppose we can try," said Bianca, unconvinced.

They gave the babies a bath, combed their hair, starched the bundles and put them into a wicker basket which they used to keep their knitting things. Aglaia wrote a label for the basket:

> We are four abandoned orphans. Please take pity on us.

"Orphans my foot!" Bianca said. "The parents who wanted them aren't dead. In fact, at this very moment, they might be thinking *they*'ve been orphaned, because the babies they wanted never arrived. But do you really believe this story about mail orders?"

"Certainly not. Who knows how many lies those storks told us…"

"So there are no grieving parents after all. The storks just invented these babies. Invented babies don't need parents."

"Yes, but they still need to be fed, and their nappies changed," Aglaia remarked. "So let's call them 'orphans', even if it isn't true. Who knows, perhaps Mr Beccaris Brullo will feel pity and take them off our hands."

But Mr Beccaris Brullo wasn't the kind of man who felt pity easily.

They placed the basket on his doorstep and knocked on the door, retreating to watch what happened from behind a branch.

The old man opened the door, saw the babies, picked up the label and read it.

"Well, you don't say!" he exclaimed, and he gave a kick to the basket which sent it flying down from the branch. Poor little newborn mites! As if they hadn't been knocked about enough that day by the storks! Aglaia caught hold of an ivy creeper and swung swiftly down through the tree to catch them before they hit the ground.

"It's obviously going to be up to us to look after them!" exclaimed Bianca with an air of resignation.

So now they needed to find four names for the new arrivals.

Bianca wanted to call the twins Wolfram and Tungsten, but then they discovered these were the names of a mineral, so they dropped the idea.

"A pity," said Bianca. "They sounded like German names."

They also decided against using any of the names of their uncles and aunts; there were so many of these, and there were only four babies! Those whose names weren't chosen might feel jealous. Aglaia wanted to call the two boys Tarzan and Mowgli.

"And what if they're scared of the slightest thing? After all, they might grow up to be cowards." Bianca remarked.

In the end Aglaia took an opera book from the shelf and spent two days reading all the names in the most famous operas in order to find some she liked. Each time she came across one she wrote it down in a notebook. She chose these kinds of names: Rigoletto, Eliogabalo, Rodrigo, Ferrando, Leporello, Gurnemanz, Oroveso...

Actually the names she liked best were Contralto, Soprano, Appassionato, Adagietto e Vivacissimo, but Bianca pointed out to her that these weren't names of opera characters but of types of voices and tempos.

"Why can't you give a child the name of a singing voice or tempo?" Aglaia protested.

They argued a bit, but eventually decided on a compromise. The twins would be called Papagena and Ormindo, while the other two children would be named Andantino and Accelerando.

Who knows if the babies liked their names? But they didn't cry any more than they usually did when Bianca and Aglaia used them.

But now they needed to organize themselves properly so that bringing up all these babies didn't disrupt too much the lives of their two adoptive mothers.

A Party in the Tree

The first thing the two friends did was to obtain some earplugs in case the four babies cried all through the night. They weren't prepared to give up their sleep on their account. But the four bawled their heads off during the day as well, and it wasn't possible to go around all the time wearing earplugs.

"What if they're crying because they're hungry?" wondered Aglaia after a while.

Bianca was doubtful. Officially the babies were not yet born. Who'd ever heard of a baby who needed to eat before being born?

"But who knows if the storks were telling the truth?" she asked. "They might already be six months old and able to chew toffee."

In any case, they decided to acquire some milk-bearing animal who could feed the babies. They had no intention of spending their time sterilizing bottles and mashing food. Keeping a cow was out of the question: it would have been too heavy for any of the branches. Aglaia wanted a wolf, like the one which had suckled Romulus and Remus.

"Oh, perfect," said Bianca sarcastically. "That way they'll grow up to spend their lives quarrelling with each other. A goat would be better. Zeus was suckled by a goat."

"At the risk they'd start chucking thunderbolts down from the tree and scorching the grass?"

They argued for a couple of hours, the four children screaming at the top of their voices all the while.

"Come on, let's not quarrel," Bianca said eventually. "It's just this racket that is getting on our nerves."

"In any case," remarked Aglaia, "where are we going to find a wolf or a goat round here? So it's pointless to argue."

They looked down at the field. There was a flock of sheep.

"No, you're not going to bring them up on sheep's milk!" exclaimed Bianca indignantly. "They'd turn into cretins. Sheep are bywords for silliness, after all."

"What about a fox?' Aglaia suggested.

"Perhaps. But I don't think a fox would be prepared to take on nursing responsibilities."

All the while time was passing, and the babies were growing hungrier and hungrier. They tried to get them to drink some water from the tap, but the babies weren't deceived.

"If they don't stop shrieking, I'll throw them off the tree," grumbled Bianca. But at that moment Amedeo turned up to save the situation.

Amedeo had been in love for some time with a female St Bernard called Dorotea. She was a large white dog with brown and tawny patches, and she lived in a barn behind the hill. Alas, their love was thwarted, since Dorotea couldn't climb the tree, so the two were never able to meet.

"Yes, she seems a very nice, trustworthy kind of dog. Just the right kind to bring up four babies," said Bianca, when Amedeo pointed out his beloved sitting at a distance. "But I hope she won't ask for a huge salary!"

Dorotea turned out to have modest expectations. So she came and positioned herself at the bottom of the tree, while Bianca let down four ropes and Aglaia descended to secure each of them to Dorotea's paws. Then, with a lot of effort, they started to pull her up, and finally hauled her onto the platform.

The babies immediately took to her milk, and after feeding they all fell straight asleep. Bianca gave a sigh of relief and started to look for something she could make into four cradles.

In the meantime, Dorotea was washing the four little infants, licking them from top to toe with her enormous wet pink tongue – which meant that Aglaia had to wash all of them all over again under the shower.

Bianca returned with two huge coconuts, which she picked on one of the south-facing branches. She split them in two and made the four halves into cradles into which the four babies fitted just as snugly as could be. Perhaps they were a bit too tight… but better like that: it meant they were warm and they couldn't move about too freely and start causing a ruckus. Then the two stretched two pieces of string and a pulley between two branches which were quite a distance from each other and attached the cradles to the string, creating a kind of cable-car system. The four babies in their cradles could go up and down the whole day long without anyone having to bother to take them out for walks. As for rocking them, the wind would do that.

And when there wasn't any wind? Then Prunilde could help out. Like all cats she was fascinated by moving objects; she would spend hours sitting on a branch waiting for the cradles to pass in front of her, and she would give each a gentle tap as it went by.

The arrival of the babies was one novelty too far for Mr Beccaris Brullo. He wasn't fond of children, and he found newborn babies particularly irritating. And in any case, as one of the residents, he had not been consulted. He therefore asked for an extraordinary meeting to be held at which he could vote against this new development. He kicked up such a fuss and annoyed Bianca so much that she told him to stop going on about it, otherwise she'd kick him so hard he'd end up where the storks had gone.

Having arranged matters so conveniently, the two friends decided to hold a big party in order to present the new arrivals to society.

They invited their friends and relatives, grandparents, aunts and uncles. But how could they let all these people come to the tree without their finding out the way there?

"Don't worry about that," said Aglaia. "Last year I did a course in magic, and I know lots of conjuring tricks. And not just conjuring – I can hypnotize people as well."

"Wonderful!" Bianca exclaimed. "That means we can invite all the guests to your grandmother's house. Then we'll make them fall asleep and bring them here without any of them noticing what's happened."

So it was all agreed. Elegant invitation cards were sent out, and about twenty friends and relatives gathered in the sitting room in Aglaia's grandmother's house. There were eight adults, eleven children and a two-year old toddler. They immediately started to ask Aglaia to "do some magic": "Come on, Aglaia. Show us some spells!"

Aglaia put on a top hat, like a magician, and asked her grandmother to come up to the table, where she'd placed her magic equipment. Then she got her to lie down in a box with only her head and feet visible at either end and started to saw it in half.

"Oooh! Oooh!" her grandmother started to wail.

"You haven't forgotten to ask her to bend her knees and put false feet at the other end," Bianca whispered in Aglaia's ear.

"I think I might have done" replied Aglaia, again in a whisper, so the others wouldn't hear.

"Then you must be really sawing her in half," said Bianca.

"So what?" said Aglaia. "She is rather fat, after all. It won't do her any harm to lose a bit of weight."

"But you're sawing across her, not down her, you silly sausage!" whispered Bianca. "You won't get a slimmer grandmother, you'll end up with two half-grandmothers, both even fatter than she was…"

"Oooh! Oooh!" exclaimed Aglaia. She didn't know what to do, since she didn't want to reveal her secrets to the audience.

"Oooh! Oooh!" groaned her grandmother as the edge of the saw started to tickle her tummy.

Luckily Bianca had a bright idea. "Why not hypnotize the audience now?" she suggested.

Aglaia immediately began to intone, in a monotonous and persuasive voice: "Ladies and gentlemen, are you feeling sleepy? Yes, you are feeling very sleepy. Very very sleepy..."

And – can you believe it? – in two or three minutes all of them were snoring away, quite dead to the world.

After that, it was easy to transport them to the tree. When, on arrival, they woke up, they were amazed to find themselves there. But they really admired the house. And they ate and drank and played games and danced. In short, they had a whale of a time.

As evening came on, there was a problem with lighting. The two friends didn't keep an electric ray in the bathtub like Mr Beccaris Brullo (by the way, what's become of him? How come he wasn't complaining that he hadn't been consulted about the party? What was he up to now?).

But as luck would have it, the tree was full of glow-worms, who were asked, very politely, if they would form into clusters and position themselves around the house. What wonderful lighting! It made for a magical atmosphere. But the height of success for the glow-worms was when they decided to group themselves in Aglaia's hair and around her neck, forming a crown and necklace of shimmering diamonds – and, even better, moving all the time. The party was going with

a swing when Bianca suddenly exclaimed: "Oh, how silly of me to forget! We invited all of you to celebrate something extraordinary. We've been partying for two hours and we haven't even mentioned it yet."

"Really? An important piece of news? Oh, what could it be?" all the guests started to ask, their curiosity aroused.

Then Dorotea – who up until that point had been trying to keep the children quiet by licking and rocking them, with Prunilde's assistance – made her entrance, holding Andantino by the nape of the neck, just as she would have done with one of her own puppies. She put him down at Aglaia's feet and returned to collect Ormindo. Prunilde wanted to help out too, but she was too small to carry a baby twice her weight.

So Dorotea made the journey four times, while Prunilde escorted her with an air of self-importance.

All the guests began to compliment the two friends on how beautiful and healthy-looking the four babies were, and how they could see the resemblance to this or that relative, just as people usually do.

"But none of us knows who the relatives are!" thought Aglaia. "People are really strange."

Bianca gave out special gold and silver sweets; everyone hugged and greeted each other, just like at a New Year's party. One or two people were so overcome with emotion they started to cry. But Aglaia's grandmother, still offended because her granddaughter had tried to saw her in half, complained: "I've never seen four such dirty-looking children in my life!"

"You're always criticizing" Aglaia told her. "Be careful what you say or you'll upset Dorotea."

Bianca was about to intervene to stop the two arguing when they suddenly heard a great racket coming from the top of the tree.

The Tenant's Curse

At the noise Aglaia's grandmother swallowed the gold sweet she was sucking. It went down the wrong way and she started to choke. They had to hold her head down from one of the branches while thumping her on the back until she managed to spit the sweet out.

Aglaia ran to fetch the gun. Bianca tore her hair out: "Mr Beccaris Brullo! The wretched man! I might have known it!"

The noise had indeed been caused by Mr B.B. Indignant that he had not been invited to the party, he decided to roll old tin cans down the branch while singing a bawdy song at the top of his voice.

Bianca, wishing to avoid any embarrassment in front of the guests, attempted to remedy the unpleasant situation by inviting, albeit belatedly, the grumpy old man.

"Would you like to come down and have a slice of cake?" she asked him in a kindly voice. "I was going to invite you yesterday, but you weren't at home."

"Yesterday I was in bed all day, so don't tell lies," Mr Beccaris Brullo brusquely replied as he landed on the lower platform with an ungainly jump. "And even if you had invited me, I wouldn't have come. I've got nothing in common with the rabble you've invited. Your friends!"

Hearing themselves called "rabble", the guests took offence. Just who did he think he was, this boorish old man? One of them spat an olive stone in his face. Another thumbed his nose at him behind a glass of Coca-Cola. But Mr Beccaris Brullo loftily ignored such provocations. He was above such trivialities now. He had prepared his revenge.

He placed himself right in the middle of the guests, took up a threatening stance with his legs astride and, pointing at the four babies with his index finger, thundered: "This is my baptismal gift! These little snivellers will prick themselves with a safety pin and fall asleep for one hundred years!"

The guests reacted in various ways to the curse.

Most of them were upset because none of them had thought about bringing a baptismal present for the babies. After all, they hadn't even known the occasion was intended to be a baptismal party.

Others were scandalized. "What coarse manners! These two young women" (they meant Bianca and Aglaia) "certainly associate with some undesirable people!"

Aglaia's grandmother said: "This story sounds familiar. Perhaps I read it in a book? Oh, my poor old brain. I must be losing my memory."

Bianca said to Aglaia: "Quick! Run and find a safety pin! If it really works and these four grizzlers sleep for the next one hundred years, just think of the peace and quiet we'll have!"

"Yes, you're right!" replied Aglaia. "They wouldn't cry during the night any more and, what's more, we could give poor Dorotea a holiday. She's completely worn out and needs one."

But it's very hard to find a safety pin in a tree – until one of the guests very generously offered the one he was using to hold up his trousers, since he'd forgotten to put his belt and braces on.

But just as she was about to prick the babies with it, Bianca's courage failed her. After all, the party was really being held for them, the poor little mites. And then Mr Beccaris Brullo's curse was a complete piece of nonsense. When have you ever heard of one of your neighbours casting a spell?

Only Dorotea remained put out by Bianca's decision. It meant she'd go on having sleepless nights trying to rock the howling babies to sleep, though it's true she had Prunilde's sterling assistance.

When he saw that his curse had not had the slightest effect on anyone, Mr Beccaris Brullo assumed an attitude of haughty indifference and threw himself on the buffet, cramming down so many savouries and cakes that on the following day they had to use the pulley to lift him back to his house.

But the incident marked the end of the party. The guests were tired and wanted to go to bed. So it was very easy for Aglaia to hypnotize them all once again and take them back home, fast asleep.

By midnight everyone had left.

Bianca and Aglaia were surrounded by rubbish and empties, and Mr Beccaris Brullo was stretched out on the floor, so full of food he couldn't move. They started to clean up a bit, helped by the tree, which now and then shook off, like so many dead leaves, the crumbs and cigarette ends and bits of paper that littered the floor of the platform.

It all fell onto the field below, but it didn't create any mess. During the night the grass was full of tiny creatures, who in the twinkling of an eye cleared up all the remains of the party.

A red ant came across an emerald earring which Aglaia's mother had lost and, pleased with his find, took it off with him to his hole underground. The next day, Aglaia's mother searched her house from top to bottom for it. In fact, she's still looking.

Before going to bed inside the trunk, Bianca inspected her part of the tree. Aglaia was asleep, curled up in her hanging bed. Dorotea was snoring in her basket, while Amedeo guarded her. Prunilde was snoozing stretched out along a branch while keeping one eye open on the babies in their cradles, which gently rocked back and forth in the breeze. If they weren't actually sleeping, at least they were quiet.

Bianca thought back to the day when she and Aglaia had moved to the tree because of their desire to have a new house, different from those where people normally lived. Back then she could certainly never have foreseen that one day their new residence would be quite so crowded.

"We'd better watch out," thought Bianca. "At this rate we'll have a family to maintain!"

The Children Change Diet

It was a wet winter morning. Bianca and Aglaia had put the walls up all round the house, making sure they fitted well so no rain or draughts got in. The tree also lent a hand, closing its branches together and stretching out its larger leaves above and around their house, so that it was well protected against the downpours.

It was cosy inside. The two friends had arranged the walls to form one large room. That morning all the members of their strange household were present.

"This way it's easier to keep an eye on things," said Aglaia.

She had brought the piano and put it in a corner of the room, and she sat at it trying to compose some music resembling the sound of the rain on the leaves.

"But that's cheating!" Bianca protested. "That way you're just copying."

"Not at all. I'm looking for inspiration," replied Aglaia, listening out for the sound of the raindrops. "I'd like to play music like this in the middle of summer, perhaps on a really hot day. Just think how refreshing it would be!"

Bianca was busy sewing clothes for the children out of the large yellow leaves which had fallen from the tree in the autumn.

Dorotea was snoring in the middle of the room with the children clustered asleep round her, clinging to her coat. Amedeo was staring curiously out of the window – not that there was much to see: just leaves, then more leaves, and the raindrops, which seemed to fascinate him. "How can they all be the same? How can they all go in the same direction?" he seemed to be thinking.

Prunilde, in the meantime, was hiding under the piano to stalk a spider. But after a bit she got bored and went over to sniff the children as they slept, tickling them with her whiskers.

One of them woke up – Papagena, the little twin girl. She pushed herself up to sit. Then, holding on to Prunilde's neck, she lifted herself to her feet and took a couple of unsteady steps.

"Oh, look," exclaimed Aglaia happily. "She's learnt to walk!"

"And about time too!" replied Bianca. "They must be twelve months old by now, give or take a bit." She turned to Papagena. "Come here, sweetheart, come over here. Let go of Prunilde and try to walk on your own" – and she stretched out her arms towards her. But Prunilde was proud of being the nurse and led the little girl to the other side of the room.

"Don't you think," Aglaia observed, "that they seem to have lost weight recently?"

"So you've noticed too?" Bianca agreed. "It's a bit worrying... Dorotea too seems to be behaving a bit oddly these last few days. Perhaps she's not feeling well."

At the sound of her name, the huge dog woke up, stretched herself, yawned and got to her feet, shaking the three children off her. They rolled along the floor crying. With a casual air she sauntered round the room, sniffing in the corners and giving an affectionate lick to Amedeo. Then, as discreetly as possible, she edged the door open and slipped out under the rain.

"What was I saying? " Bianca remarked. "Do you think it's normal behaviour to go out in this weather?"

But Aglaia, quick as a flash, had slipped off the piano stool and grabbed her raincoat with the hood. Then she too was gone, to follow Dorotea.

Aglaia looked up in the direction of the rustling leaves. She saw the dog climbing from branch to branch, going higher and higher. She set off behind her, trying to make no noise.

Climbing and climbing, finally Dorotea came to a halt, much higher than Mr Beccaris Brullo's house. Aglaia, hidden among the branches, saw her approach, on the tip of her paws, a large nest.

"Oh, no!" Aglaia sighed. "She's been led astray by that wicked Prunilde! It's one thing for a cat to hunt birds' eggs. But for a dog! That takes the biscuit!"

Dorotea sniffed the nest and gave it a little tap and then… she sat down on top of it. Wrapped up in her yellow raincoat, Aglaia watched her, bewildered.

All the while the rain just kept on falling. The poor dog's fur was completely sodden, but she went on sitting on the eggs, oblivious to the rain. The nest – it has to be admitted – was a bit crooked and was unusually large.

Eventually Dorotea got up and scampered away, back down the tree. So Aglaia carefully went over to the nest and, moving the leaves that covered it, saw five strange-looking eggs. They were a lot bigger than ordinary hen's eggs. They were dark, with splodges of yellow and brown.

"I wonder which bird laid them?" thought Aglaia. "And who knows why Dorotea has taken to sitting on them… It's lucky she hasn't squashed them!" Then she thought: "Such a big nest must belong to a very big bird. The eggs too – I've never seen such large ones.

Could they be eagle's eggs? Just as well the mother didn't come back while that silly creature was sitting on them. Then we'd have been in real trouble!"

And she climbed back down the tree. But she decided to say nothing about what she had seen to Bianca, because she didn't want to worry her.

The next day, the weather was fine. All four children were now beginning to take their first steps, and Prunilde and Dorotea had their hands full supporting them or running to pick them up and comfort them whenever they fell. Prunilde was purring with pride, but Dorotea, despite the novelty of the occasion, still managed to slip away again.

Aglaia had been waiting for this, and she immediately followed her. In fact, when she was on the branches, she took a short cut only she knew and, climbing up very quickly, got to the eagle's nest before Dorotea arrived. She took another look at the eggs: there were five of them, as big as grapefruit. Then she hid herself in the usual spot.

Dorotea arrived, stepping carefully and looking round suspiciously, with her nose quivering with excitement. She reached the nest, sniffed all round it with a worried air, and then, just like the day before, sat down on it.

"How irresponsible can you get?" thought Aglaia. "Why on earth does she do it? I must protect her, in case the mother eagle comes back. "And she got her catapult ready.

But no eagle came, and once again, after a while, Dorotea got up and left. Aglaia approached the nest. She had to hold on hard to the edges to stop herself falling over with surprise. There were six eggs inside the nest. Six!

She picked up two and put them in her pockets and then climbed quickly down to the house.

Bianca was on her own, because she'd sent the children to play in the field, so they could practise walking on firm ground, watched over by the animals.

Aglaia took out the eggs and showed them to her.

"What's got into you? You can't go around taking eggs from nests!" Bianca scolded her absent-mindedly.

"But take a good look at them! Just look! What kind of eggs are they?"

"Hmm... I've no idea. They certainly don't come from a canary! It must be a really large bird."

"Birds my foot! These are a dog's eggs."

And that's exactly what they were. Poor Dorotea had laid them. She'd now been in the tree so long that she was changing from the dog she had been. A few feathers had grown among her fur; you didn't notice them because St Bernards have very shaggy coats. One fine day she'd suddenly felt the overwhelming urge to go and build a nest.

It had been far from easy to build one. The poor dog had had to work with her clumsy paws and her large tongue; she didn't have a bird's beak or its slender feet. And she was also ashamed of herself, so didn't dare to ask anyone for help or advice.

That's why the nest looked a bit odd, rather too solid, awkwardly constructed and slightly crooked, with corners and a roof like a kennel. But that didn't matter: when Dorotea came to lay her first egg, the nest was ready for it.

"I wonder if when they hatch they'll be puppies with wings?" Aglaia asked, intrigued.

"No, surely not," replied Bianca. "I don't think these eggs are for hatching. From what you've told me, I think Dorotea went there just to lay the eggs, not to hatch them. They're probably only good for eating."

"They certainly look as if they'd make a great omelette!" said Aglaia.

"Now I understand!" Bianca exclaimed, hitting her forehead. "That's why the babies have lost so much weight! Dorotea can't have any more milk for them. Poor little things – if we hadn't found out, they might have starved to death. Dorotea's days as a wet nurse are over, I fear."

"That's no big deal," said Aglaia. "It's time they were weaned anyway. Now they can eat everything."

And when the children came in from their walk tired and famished and ran straight to Dorotea to feed, Bianca and Aglaia swept them up and seated them on four high chairs in front of four steaming plates.

"No milk for you today!" said Bianca. "Today there's a change of menu! Today we're eating omelettes!"

Infant Lispings

Dorotea might have had no more milk, but to compensate she was laying an egg every day. It was large enough to feed the four hungry children, who started to grow and put on weight by the minute. Now they were able to walk well; in fact, they were much better than either Bianca or Aglaia at running in balance along the slenderest branches and climbing up to the top of the tree, like monkeys. However, they hadn't yet spoken a word.

"Perhaps they're dumb," said Aglaia with a worried air.

Bianca on the other hand feared that at any moment all four of them would start to sing like birds. After all, they'd arrived with the storks.

"They're more likely to start barking," Aglaia observed, "seeing they've been brought up by Dorotea."

But it turned out to be Prunilde with her cat language who'd had the most influence on them.

One day, Aglaia was cuddling Accelerando in her arms – he really was such a sweet little lad – when he rubbed his head against her chin and said: "Miaow!"

"Oh my goodness!" exclaimed Aglaia. "So he can speak, after all. But it's not exactly what I was expecting to hear. Go on, say 'mama', little one, or 'dum-dum' or 'moo-moo', like other children."

"Miaow!" Accelerando repeated, with a puzzled expression. He was so cute that Aglaia just had to stroke his hair.

At that, much to her consternation, the little boy started to purr. "Prrrr... prrrrr..." he went, throwing his little arms round her neck.

"Help!" cried Aglaia. "Bianca, quick, come here! We must do something, now."

But, instead of Bianca, Dorotea padded in slowly, with the other three children holding on to her sides and tail.

"Now let's hear what the rest of you have learnt to say. So? Come on, Ormindo, say 'mama', 'ma-ma', 'MA-MA'..." Aglaia pleaded.

"Miaow! Gnau!" Ormindo angrily squealed. He didn't want to talk, and it annoyed him to be spoken to in that tone of voice.

"Oh, no, not you as well. And what about you, Andantino, my little pet? What have you got to say to me?"

Andantino let go of Dorotea's tail and fell with a bump onto his bottom.

"Gnaoooo!" he wailed.

"Miaow, miaow, miaow!" Accelerando started to repeat, so as not to be left out.

"Now look, Dorotea, aren't you ashamed of yourself? Aglaia asked. "It's you who've been responsible for bringing these children up. How come you let that cat have such an influence over them?"

Dorotea looked at Aglaia dejectedly. She wanted to say sorry, but clearly didn't dare say anything. Two or three times she opened her mouth to say something, but no sound emerged; in the meantime, the children continued to miaow all around her. Finally, in an apologetic tone, she managed to say: "Cheep."

She no longer knew how to bark.

"Heavens above, what kind of tree is this? It's like the Tower of Babel!" Aglaia shrieked as she ran to where the branches divided, dropped down into the hollow trunk and out through the secret little door, slamming it behind her.

Later that evening, Bianca tried to reason with her. "Don't take on so about it. They weren't doing it to annoy you. If anything, it's our fault. We've neglected them too much. What do you expect after all the time they've spent with dogs and cats? I'll take over from now on. I'll give them two hours of conversation classes every day."

But it's not so easy to have conversations with children who are so little.

The next day, Bianca got them all to sit in their high chairs, all lined up in front of her, and began: "Today we're going to talk about Eskimo philosophy."

"Miaow?" said Papagena enquiringly.

"Gnau, gnau!" added Ormindo, and started to laugh.

"Stop it! From today you're going to sing a different tune!" Bianca exclaimed severely. "If I hear you miaow once more, I'll throw you off the tree!"

The children started to laugh and miaow all at the same time.

"Stop that! I won't tell you again!" Bianca repeated angrily. "Otherwise I'll fetch Mr Beccaris Brullo."

At this dreaded name the children suddenly fell silent.

"Now then," continued Bianca in a milder voice. "What would you like to tell me today? No miaowing, remember!"

There was a moment's silence, then Accelerando put his hand up.

"Go on, sweetheart, tell me what you want to say."

"Bow-wow!" uttered Accelerando, blushing with pleasure at not having miaowed. Bianca was speechless.

"Bow-wow, bow-wow, woof woof!" Ormindo joined in.

"Caw, caw, caw," Papagena croaked.

"Uh, uuuh, uuuuh," Andantino bleated.

"Children, children! That's not what I meant, not what I meant at all! I see this calls for drastic action," Bianca said with a decisive air. "From now on please be so kind as not to speak for several days and just listen to what I have to say to you."

The children quickly closed their mouths and listened attentively.

"Oh good Heavens, now what shall I talk to them about?" Bianca anxiously thought. "What can I say to four little children so they won't become bored?"

"What about reciting a poem to them?" suggested Aglaia, who in the meantime had joined them.

"You're right. Now pay attention, my little darlings! Listen carefully and try to remember.

"Twinkle, twinkle, little star,
How I wonder what you are!
Up above the world so high,
Like a diamond in the sky..."

The children hung on her every word. A contrite Prunilde – she was sitting near one of the high chairs – was also following the words.

"Could you take over, please?" Bianca asked Aglaia when, after three hours, her voice finally gave way.

"Hickory, dickory, dock,
The mouse ran up the clock…"

Aglaia began. It seemed the children would never get tired of listening.

For a week the two friends took turns at giving the children language lessons. The children didn't make a sound. But they listened with rapt attention.

While all this was going on, Amedeo, who was worried by the strange transformation taking place in his beloved, had persuaded Dorotea to let him give her lessons in "canine re-education". The two dogs would retire to some large and deserted branch, and Amedeo would bark now this way, now that, now in one kind of tone, now in another, patiently asking Dorotea to copy him each time.

"Bow… cheep!" said Dorotea. "Woof… trill, trill, trill! Grrr… peep, peep, peep!" In short, all she could do now was sing and trill and chirp. Barking was quite beyond her. And the stiff feathers growing along her front paws were now quite clearly visible.

Amedeo was dismayed. "What will become of our love for each other?" he lamented in dog language.

"Cheep, cheep," a disconsolate Dorotea replied.

On the ninth day, Bianca said to the four children: "Now let's see if you've learnt anything. Even the simplest word will do. You, Accelerando. Ask me for something to eat."

The little boy looked at her bewildered. "Miaow," he said very softly.

The other three started to laugh.

"Miaow!" said Prunilde scornfully.

"Come on, be brave! I know it's the first time," said Bianca encouragingly. "Try again, Accelerando, go on! What would you say if you want your din-dins? Din... din..."

"I beg your pardon," an unknown voice suddenly said, "but I wonder if you would be so kind as to provide some alimentation for my nourishment?"

Bianca jumped out of her skin. "What?! Who said that?"

"Excuse me," the voice repeated, "might it be possible for you to arrange an appropriate repast so that I may sate my insistent appetite?"

"Who said that?" Bianca asked again. She was a little scared, since she could see that none of the children had even opened their mouths. "Who's speaking?" she insisted.

Out from under Papagena's high chair Prunilde proudly emerged, holding her tail triumphantly erect.

"It was I who gave utterance to these polished expressions," said the cat. "I wished to make clear to you how excellently well I have imbibed the fruits of your teaching."

"Heavens above! Aglaia, come here!" Bianca called, quite beside herself. "After hearing all that poetry, Prunilde has learnt how to talk!"

"Yes, that is indeed the case. You are correct. It is precisely as you say," said the cat with great satisfaction.

"And so what? What's the harm?" Aglaia remarked as she swung in on an ivy creeper. "It just goes to show what good teachers we are."

"But the children have learnt nothing!"

"But that's not true, as you can hear! Your thinking is deceived, I fear," said Ormindo, standing up on his chair.

"Oh yes, we've learnt your lesson well... Just hear us speak, clear as a bell," added Andantino, stumbling over the words in his haste.

"Well, just listen to that!" Bianca said. "They've only gone and taken to speaking in verse!"

"We listened hard as you spoke, Miss... That's how we learnt to rhyme like this," Papagena explained.

"But can't you talk normally?" asked Aglaia.

"No, by faith, I fear we can't. Poetic speech is all we chant," said Accelerando.

"Perhaps I should have spoken in prose as well during the lessons," sighed Bianca. "But I'm afraid now it's too late."

"Don't worry," Aglaia comforted her. "At least they can make themselves understood. And, after all, they're invented children, as we've always known. So there's no harm done if invented children talk in verse."

"Exactly so," Prunilde hastened to agree. "I would indeed go so far as to assert that there is nothing at all discommendable in this unaccustomed phenomenon."

The Intoxication of Flight

The day finally arrived when Dorotea, on waking up and stretching out her paws, found that her front legs were now, without a doubt, wings.

Full of apprehension, she stepped cautiously out of her basket and moved gingerly onto the branch. Amedeo was watching her full of wonder as she lifted her front paws and widened them slightly, when all of a sudden… ffrrrrr! On each side of the great St Bernard dog, rows and rows of tawny feathers, spotted with brown, spread open wide like two great fans.

Dorotea wobbled a little on the branch, thrown off balance by these unexpected appendages. Then she flapped the wings two or three times and steadied herself again. When she flapped them, the wings sounded like a gale.

"The wind must have got up," thought Bianca, as she turned over in her sleeping bag inside the hollow trunk.

Aglaia's hanging bed swung in the sudden currents of air, and she started to dream she was in a ship on a rough sea. But neither of them got up.

But the four children ran to see what was happening by pushing their coconut-shell cradles along the string to near where Dorotea's basket was. Prunilde had not been seen during the night – in search of who knows what adventures – but now she appeared at the end of a branch and observed the scene with an air of perplexity.

"By my troth!" she exclaimed, and the others as usual jumped at the sound of her voice. "By Jove!" she continued. "This precipitate concatenation of events confronts me with an arduous dilemma. How can it be that my sense of inward composure is so unduly disturbed by the inconsiderate metamorphosis of a female member of the canine species?"

Dorotea shamefacedly folded her wings and tried to hide them under her fur. But the camouflage no longer worked. Amedeo, who was distraught at the thought his beloved was now definitively transformed but wouldn't have dreamt of saying such a tactless thing, gave Prunilde a sad and disapproving look. But the cat pretended not to understand and kept her impertinent gaze fixed on Dorotea, licking her whiskers all the while.

Accelerando in the meantime had climbed out of his cradle onto the branch and ran to give the poor wretched dog a hug.

"Dorotea, don't be sad. Nothing's happened which is bad!" he said to her affectionately, stroking her wings.

"Don't be sad unnecessarily. We shall always love you dearly," Ormindo confirmed in half-rhyme, jumping astride his nurse.

Cheered up, Dorotea started to wag her tail. While this was happening, some birds – real ones – had arrived to flutter round and observe inquisitively what was going on.

Seated in her hanging cradle, Andantino clapped her little hands together: "What are we all just waiting for? Go on, Dorotea, soar!"

"Stretch your wings and leap up high. Fly up and up, you'll touch the sky!" Papagena echoed.

"Don't do it, Dorotea!" Amedeo pleaded in dog language. "It will end our relationship for ever."

"I must confess that I am most curious to see if the appearance of volant capacity will effectively correspond to an ability to maintain aerodynamic balance in the ethereal element..." murmured Prunilde, as if to herself.

Bewildered by all this conflicting advice, Dorotea flapped her wings open and shut not knowing what to do.

"Stop creating a draught!" Prunilde rebuked her. "You'll give us all stiff necks! Forsooth, settle upon a decision once and for all. Are you going to fly or not?"

"No!" barked Amedeo.

"Yes, yes, YES!" shrieked the children excitedly.

Dorotea looked round despairingly.

The birds flew round her head.

"Cheep, cheep! Cheep, cheep! Make your mind up, slowcoach!" they tweeted mockingly.

Dorotea looked down at the field below her. It seemed a long, long way away.

"Don't move!" Amedeo's sad eyes implored her.

But just at that moment a robin flew off a branch and then straight down to skim the grass at the foot of the tree. Then, with just one beat of his wings, he flew straight up again, through the leaves and out into the pure air, light and quick against the blue of the sky.

"Fly, Dorotea, fly!" cried the children, digging their hands into her coat and pushing her towards the edge of the platform.

"I'll give it a go! Cheep!" the confused dog said, and leapt into the void.

But her lack of experience meant that she forgot to open her wings in time and so plunged down, all seventy kilos (and more) of her.

Boooooooooooom! The impact with the ground was so violent the whole field shook as though there had

been an earthquake. At the spot where Dorotea landed a deep crater opened up.

"A foreseeable outcome. Fortune does not always smile on the brave!" Prunilde commented serenely, licking one of her paws. In the meantime, Bianca and Aglaia had raced to the scene.

"What 's happening? Was it a bomb? Some kind of explosion?"

"Dorotea tried to fly around… But just fell right back on the ground," a disappointed Andantino explained to them.

They had to dig for five hours before they reached Dorotea lying at the bottom of the hole. The four children sat on the edge of the crater with their buckets and spades, having the time of their lives. They were making mud pies and building castles out of the earth. Occasionally, they sifted a handful of sand through a sieve, which left little pebbles and twigs and empty snail shells…

"Dorotea can't be found," Papagena declared.

"Who knows where she's gone to ground?" Accelerando asked.

"Come on! Keep on digging round!" Ormindo urged.

"We're bound to find her, safe and sound!" Papagena concluded, encouragingly.

All the time Bianca and Aglaia were shovelling and shovelling. A mountain of soil had been heaped up next to the tree. Amedeo was helping them, scratching away with his claws just as dogs do when they want to bury a bone.

Eventually they found her, still unconscious from the impact on landing. She had opened up a hole in the earth which was ten metres deep. In order to get her back to the field, they had to tie ropes around her and pull her up, all of them heaving together on the ropes and sweating hard.

Then they threw pails of water over her to make her come round and clean the mud off her. Amedeo licked her muzzle affectionately.

"I'll love you for ever," he told her in dog talk, "even though you're so different from me now. And even though you are so silly. And even though you're good for nothing any more – you're not a dog, you're not a bird—"

"Hey, just mind what you say, won't you!" Dorotea, now completely revived, protested. She spread her large wings and flapped them threateningly.

Prunilde jumped back. "Overweening boldness is unbecoming in a well-bred cat," she remarked, to justify her retreat.

Dorotea got to her feet and attempted a couple of steps in the field.

"There's a good dog! Come on!" Aglaia encouraged her, putting ice packs on her forehead. But despite all their efforts and encouragement, the great dog could only fly a couple of inches above the ground, and even then fell back down immediately. It was obvious that her wings were simply decorative, like the wings on hens. All she could do with them was to flap them to scare off enemies, when she was in a fight, or to keep her balance on the slenderer branches. Flying was clearly out of the question.

The children were very disappointed. Amedeo, on the other hand, was feeling more cheerful.

Prunilde asked if she could have a private word with Bianca.

"An atrocious quandary afflicts my feline soul," she confessed to her. "If Dorotea belongs to the winged tribe, as a self-respecting cat I am obliged to hunt her with heart unafraid, despite her hugely disproportionate proportions. If, on the other hand, she is still a member of the canine race, then I am duty-bound to fear her and keep my distance... Could you, who are old and wise, disentangle this thorny question?"

"And just who are you calling 'old'?" Bianca retorted. "You really are the most trying of cats, with your endless crises of conscience. Why can't you just leave Dorotea in peace and mind your own business?"

"Oh, quite so! That was indeed the very solution I was cogitating," Prunilde said. "It is one which I find commodious and altogether reasonable."

Aglaia, who could hardly hide her laughter, said to Bianca: "I've had an idea. Instead of filling up the hole Dorotea has left, why don't we leave it there as a trap? After all, you never know what might happen…"

"You're right" replied Bianca. "It might come in useful if we're ever besieged."

Signals in the Night

But the first person to fall into the trap hole was Mr Beccaris Brullo.

You've probably asked yourselves lots of times whatever became of their cantankerous old neighbour, seeing he's not appeared once in the last few chapters. Well, the fact of the matter is that on the day after the party the terrible old man packed his bags and left for a long holiday. Of course, before he went, he wrapped barbed wire all round his house and told the carnivorous plant to keep a lookout for thieves.

But in his hurry he forgot all about the electric ray, who was left in the bathtub without anyone to change the water or feed him. In the dark room the poor creature languished away, while the water got smellier and he himself got thinner for lack of food.

As a fish of course he couldn't speak, and so was unable to ask for help. Nina the carnivorous plant could see him through the bathroom window and wanted to help, but didn't know how. Her tendrils weren't strong enough to prise the window open, and she couldn't call for help either. Her flowers had mouths for eating insects or beefsteak, but there wasn't a tongue or vocal cords, so she couldn't make sounds.

And in any case, as time went on, Nina herself was not best pleased with the behaviour of Mr Beccaris Brullo. "What does he think he's playing at?" she thought. "First he gets me used to a diet of beefsteak, tasty and nourishing. Then he just leaves me in the lurch without bothering to arrange any provisions, and I've got to learn to put up with eating flies again!"

But at least she managed to survive, even though it wasn't that easy.

Whereas the poor electric ray was really about to cop it. He lay curled up at the bottom of the tub waiting for death to arrive, since he now despaired of his owner ever returning.

But one night – a night in May, fragrant and mild – Aglaia was looking out of her window and counting the stars when above her, among the branches, she saw a weak light flashing on and off. At first she thought it was a glow-worm. Then she looked more closely and saw that the light was coming from Mr Beccaris Brullo's platform.

"Oh, what a pity!" she said. "Another stupid insect is just about to push his head into the teeth of the carnivorous plant!"

"Oh well, that's his lookout," said Bianca, who'd joined her at the window. "We can't run about after all the insects flying round the tree to keep them away from Nina's teeth! And in any case she too has the right to eat, now her owner has gone off".

But they couldn't take their eyes off the feeble little light. And then they realized that it came on and went off at regular intervals. It shone out very briefly, then it was dark, then another very brief flash of light. And again: light, dark, light, dark, light.

"It reminds me of something," Bianca said pensively. At the age of fifteen, she had been a cabin girl on a whaling ship.

"Glow-worms don't behave like that," agreed Aglaia.

Above them the light came on, went out, came on again, each time more feebly...

"Oh, what a fool I am! I should have realized immediately!" Bianca suddenly shouted, jumping on the window sill. "It's someone asking for help. Don't you see? A short flash, then a longer one, then another short flash. That equals stop, dash, stop. SOS! They're calling for help – they need rescuing!"

Aglaia could only just catch the last words of Bianca's explanation as her friend was already rapidly climbing up through the branches. Aglaia followed. They reached Mr Beccaris Brullo's platform together and saw that the flashing light came from the bathroom window.

"The electric ray!" shouted Aglaia. In the dark she felt something grab her in the seat of her trousers and nudge her towards the door. "There's no need to push," she said, annoyed. "I can get there by myself."

"But who's pushing?" asked Bianca, who was already wrestling with the door bolts.

Aglaia jumped forward, scared, but whoever had grabbed her wasn't letting go. It was poor Nina, who, in a generous attempt to help the dying electric ray, was giving a gentle bite, not too hard, to Aglaia's trousers, to attract her attention.

Of course it was only to be expected that despite all Bianca's efforts the door didn't open. So they had to pull the grating off from the bathroom window, using an amazingly strong ivy creeper. They found the electric ray twisting and writhing at the bottom of the now empty bathtub.

"Quick, turn on the tap!" Aglaia shouted to Bianca. "It's lucky we got here just in time!"

After they'd given the ray first aid, they carried the bathtub and its occupant down to their house to become their guest. From that time on, the fish became another one of the family.

The four children were thrilled. They spent hours gathered round the tub trying to catch the fish, splashing themselves and getting water everywhere. A worried Dorotea fluttered round them. She became very adept at picking them up by the scruff of their necks and fishing them out of the tub whenever they fell in.

As for Prunilde, she reflected on the situation for a few days and then asked to have a private word with Bianca.

"The new arrival has precipitated an anguishing dilemma in me," she began. "If I regard the electric ray as a fish, then my duty, as a self-respecting cat—"

"That's the last straw!" shouted Bianca. "I've had enough of your duty as a self-respecting cat. Your conscience is too delicate for my way of thinking. Do what you want!"

Prunilde couldn't wait to devour the fish and took the reprimand Bianca had given him as permission to go ahead.

She waited until the bathroom was empty, leapt up onto the rim of the tub and balanced herself there, waiting patiently for the electric ray to swim near enough the surface of the water for her to catch him with her claws. But she had failed to take account of two things. First, the bar of soap Papagena had wiped all along the rim of the bath. Second, the electric current the fish could produce.

After a short while, the ray came to the surface and pushed his nose out a little. Quick as a flash, Prunilde's paw shot out...

Aglaia, who was combing Dorotea's fur on a branch lower down, suddenly heard a desperate mewing: "Gnauuuuuu! Gnauuuuuuu! Gnauuuuuuu!!!"

She raced up into the bathroom, where she found Prunilde struggling in the water, with her fur all singed, spitting soap bubbles and, with piteous efforts, trying to lift herself out onto dry land.

The ray was lurking at the bottom of the tub, hardly able to contain his laughter.

"So you've had an electric shock, have you? Bad cat!" said Aglaia, grabbing Prunilde by the nape of her neck and giving her a good shake to dry her off. "Well, once bitten, twice shy, as they say!"

They had to give her a good scrubbing and hang her out on the washing line before her fur was nice and dry once more. But it took longer for it to become as soft and sleek as before.

From that day on, Prunilde steered clear of the bathtub and never spoke again of her crises of feline conscience.

All their problems seemed to be over. Life was peaceful for all the inhabitants of the tree.

Until one night Aglaia was woken by an unearthly scream together with the sound of twigs snapping and boughs breaking.

"Dorotea's tried to fly again!" she thought, getting up in haste and running to look out of the window. But the dog was on the platform, sheltering the children under her wings and clucking threateningly towards the field below. Amedeo was barking furiously in the same direction.

"It's the trap hole," said Bianca, emerging from the hollow trunk. "Someone must have fallen in. Let's go and see who it is."

They went down to the edge of the pit and dropped an electric lamp into it, attached to a rope and powered by the ray. Immediately, from the dark at the bottom of the hole, a volley of insults and swear words rose up, in a raucous grating voice.

"Beccaris Brullo!" Bianca exclaimed. "Why on earth are you coming home in the middle of the night, like a thief?"

"Why? You ask me why, you pair of female criminals!" the old man roared as he climbed up the rope. "To avoid being seen by the enemy!"

"What enemy?" asked Aglaia, astonished.

"But can't you see what's happening in front of your noses?" Beccaris Brullo yelled.

Bianca looked round, but the night was dark and the lamp didn't cast much light. Aglaia looked too, but she couldn't see anything either.

"Just keep quiet!" she said impatiently to their neighbour, who was still grumbling away. "I think I hear something odd..."

Beccaris Brullo stopped muttering, and all three of them strained to listen. They could hear quite distinctly a strange noise coming from the field... a kind of bubbling, snoring...

"It's a dragon," whispered Bianca, frozen with fear.

"No. It's someone snoring," said Aglaia.

"Yes, that's him! The enemy!" agreed Beccaris Brullo. "Luckily he's fallen asleep. And you almost made me go and wake him up by falling into your damned hole!"

"Well, at least it goes to show he sleeps like a log," said Bianca, reassured. "Let's go back to bed too. Tomorrow we'll see what the problem is."

The Great Battle

The following day Aglaia was the first to get up. She looked out of the window and saw that it was already midday.

"What a nice long sleep!" she exclaimed, stretching lazily. "We got to bed so late last night."

And she went into the kitchen to prepare breakfast.

She had a vague memory that she should be worried about something... but she didn't recall what.

"It can't be important, if I can't remember what it was," she decided. She had a glass of milk and a cup of hot chocolate and ate thirteen biscuits. Then she made some coffee and took a cup down to Bianca in the hollow of the trunk.

"Wakey-wakey, lazybones!" she greeted her cheerfully.

"So what about the enemy? Is he awake?" asked Bianca, without opening her eyes.

"The enemy! That's what I had to check!" shrieked Aglaia. She dropped the cup, spilling the coffee all over Bianca's sleeping bag, and ran up to the highest branch to look down at the field.

The enemy was already at work. It was a team of woodcutters – about ten big bearded men, armed with saws, axes, mallets and chisels. They had already cut down all the shrubs and bushes round the tree and tied the branches together in neatly arranged bundles.

They had started work at daybreak, but the two friends had not heard anything, because they always slept very heavily.

Now the woodcutters were examining the tree while their foreman made some calculations on a notepad.

"We'll need a number-ten saw…" he was muttering away. "But first we'll need to make notches round the trunk with the axe…"

"Which way does it need to fall, boss? East or west?" asked one of the men.

"Better to the east," another suggested. "That way it'll fall right onto our lorry and we won't need to load it."

"You wally! A tree this big would squash it flat. Let's do it to the west. The field's clear there. Once we've got it down, we can strip it. We can cut all the branches and boughs off and then roll the trunk onto a slide…"

"That's our tree they're talking about! They're going to cut it to pieces!" The thought gave Aglaia goose bumps. She flew like an arrow to Bianca, then to the animals and the children, and then to Beccaris Brullo.

"We must defend ourselves!" she screamed. "We must be ready for them!"

So, when the four woodcutters who had to make the first notches in the trunk approached the tree to start their work, they were met with a thick hail of walnuts and hazelnuts which rained down on them and knocked them out.

"You idiots! Getting caught by squirrels!" their boss shouted.

It was in fact the four children, jumping from branch to branch like monkeys as they kept an eye on the men below and took aim.

"Get up, you bunch of sapheads!" the foreman ordered.

But a prickly chestnut case hit him right on his big nose and stuck there.

"Aaargh!" he exclaimed, trying to pull it out. Just then, five prickly pears whistled past his ears, while a sixth hit him square on the forehead.

"Blasted squirrels!" he shouted. "We must get these pests out of the tree. Light a fire! The smoke will drive them out."

But Bianca was manning the taps, and as soon as the flames were sufficiently high, Mr Ceglie's plumbing released jets and sprays of water in such a violent downpour that not only were the flames extinguished,

but the men's encampment was completely washed away.

"So it's not squirrels up there, then!" shouted the foreman. He gathered his men together to organize a full-scale onslaught.

Five minutes later, they rushed towards the tree yelling and brandishing their axes.

Bang! Bang! Bang! Beccaris Brullo's shotgun hit seven men in the hands and feet. The eighth, who was running away, got shot in the backside.

"Once more unto the breach, brave soldiers!" roared the enraged foreman.

The men regrouped around the trunk. Beccaris Brullo had no shot left, but luckily Aglaia had found her old catapult and hit each of them with unfailing aim, while the four children ran up and down to supply her with large coconuts. Struck in the chest, the men kept tumbling to the ground and then getting up to continue their assault.

The battle continued until sundown without the tree receiving even so much as scratch. As dark fell, the enemy troops retreated behind the hill to hold a council of war.

The tree's defenders too met to decide on their battle plan.

"We need to do something extraordinary," said Aglaia, "something which will put the wind up them and drive them away for ever."

In the middle of the night Bianca heard the tread of feet at the bottom of the tree. The enemy had returned with ladders. Instead of just trying to cut the tree down, they'd decided to take the defenders by surprise, asleep in their houses.

One of the woodcutters started to climb the ladder. He was halfway up when a soft black ball suddenly landed on his shoulder. He heard a demonic voice whisper something incomprehensible in his ear, and sharp claws dug into his neck.

"Help! It's the Devil!" he shrieked.

But it was Prunilde, who, extremely pleased with herself, leapt onto another of the attackers. In the pitch dark the man heard a soft voice in his ear: "Distinguished sir, would you care to desist from this heinous enterprise?"

"The Devil!" he too cried out in terror, and fell off the ladder in his amazement. Amedeo was waiting for the enemy on the ground and sank his teeth into their calves or backsides. In short, the glory of that first hour belonged to the cat and dog.

Once more the foreman gathered his men together to rally their spirits.

"Let's leave it, boss! The tree's haunted!" the burly bearded troops pleaded with him.

"Nonsense! We came here to cut wood, and that's what we're going to do!" the woodman insisted.

But up above, among the branches, a bright light came on and the lower platform appeared transformed into a stage. The electric ray was working flat out to keep the stage lights on. In the middle of the stage stood Aglaia, wearing her conjurer's costume, and next to her the little table with her magic tricks...

"Ladies and gentlemen!" she said in a coaxing voice.

"Hey, watch it, who are you calling 'ladies'? No females round here," said one of the woodcutters.

"Ssh! Let's see what she's going to say," said another, digging him in the ribs.

"Ladies and gentlemen, silence please!" repeated Aglaia. "I ask you to pay the utmost attention. You are about to witness the most extraordinary sight!" And she took her top hat off and showed everyone it was empty.

"She thinks she can pull the wool over our eyes?" said one of the woodman scoffingly.

"It'll be some rabbit or dove she pulls out, you'll see," said another.

"Oh yes, as if that's going to impress us!" sneered the foreman.

But they all went on watching, because everyone likes to watch conjuring tricks, if only in the hope of finding out how they're done.

In the expectant hush, Aglaia slowly put her hand into the hat... and drew out... an enormous St Bernard dog. Dorotea!

"That's quite something! A dog! and a really huge one too!" one of the woodcutters remarked in admiration.

"Pooh! That kind of thing doesn't impress me!" said the foreman.

But he'd hardly finished speaking when Dorotea unfurled her huge wings and stood on the edge of the platform.

"Fly, Dorotea, fly!" shrieked the children. And Dorotea launched herself into the air.

"Help! She's going to fall on us! She'll flatten us!" screamed the terrified men.

But Dorotea, with one supreme effort, managed to lift herself, circled the tree flying close to the leaves and then nosedived towards the enemy, barking (yes, barking!!!) menacingly.

This was too much for the woodcutters. They took to their heels, pulling their lorry, saws, axes and chisels with them. Dorotea circled them, flapping her wings and barking, as far as the hill.

"What did I tell you?" said Aglaia to Bianca afterwards. "You need to feel a strong emotion if you're going to try to fly."

"Dorotea's off to fly!

"It's so beautiful to see!

"Like a cloud she floats on high!

"Or like a bird, soaring free!" the children chanted happily.

Amedeo said: "But she's rediscovered her true voice. She chased off our enemies with her barking. Dorotea can bark again! That's the most important thing!" But he was speaking in dog language, so no one, apart from his beloved, could understand him.

Afterword

In about the mid-1970s, I became great friends with a little girl who was the daughter of friends who lived nearby. She was called Aglaia, and when I first got to know her she was three years old. She was an only child, and she and I spent a lot of time together. I was her babysitter, I took her to the theatre and cinema, I cut her hair, I asked her for advice on the TV programmes which at the time I was working on for the RAI. Aglaia was a serious and thoughtful little girl, and talking with her about all sorts of subjects was a real pleasure. We spent a lot of time in the public park near her home. We would play with her dolls arranged between the roots of a large tree which grew near the swings and slides. Aglaia was six when there was the great energy crisis and no cars were allowed in the city for many days. It was delightful to go out together on our bikes or on our rollerskates without any risk of being knocked down by a car.

But her grandmother wasn't very happy about our excursions and thought that I at least should behave more "seriously", seeing I was an adult. Aglaia was going to infant school and was learning to read and write. So one weekend I wrote a long story for her in which she was the heroine on rollerskates, accompanied by her grandmother and an imaginary animal called a "drogopild". Among the other characters there were other of her relatives and several of our mutual friends.

I had already published several books by this time, but I wrote a single copy of this work for my little friend. I illustrated it myself and sewed the pages together with needle and thread, and I prepared a coloured cover for the book. Three years went by when one day I found in my postbox a letter Aglaia had sent me (though she lived just three blocks away and I saw her almost every day). She'd written the letter at school while at a loose end, because she had to wait for her classmates to finish an exercise, and in it she said: "Do you remember when you asked me if I'd like to live in a tree? I've thought about the idea all these years, and every night I've dreamt of going to live in a tree with you."

How could I reply to such a beautiful letter? I wrote this book, and in it I put all our fantasies and all our conversations, our animals, our toys, our friends and family. The hapless plumber, for example, really existed, and so did Prunilde the cat. And Aglaia's grandmother was indeed so plump that if you'd cut her in two lengthwise she would have become more elegant.

Unlike the story with the drogopild, I offered this book to a publisher, who brought it out. But Aglaia's grandmother was offended with the way I'd described her, and for a long time refused to talk to me.

Born in Sassari, Bianca Pitzorno lives and works in Milan. Much loved by young readers, she has published over forty books for children and young people since 1970, many of them bestsellers. Today Bianca Pitzorno is considered Italy's foremost children's writer, and her novels have been translated into French, German, Spanish, Greek, Polish, Hungarian, Korean and Japanese. She is a UNICEF Goodwill Ambassador.

Treasure Island, by Robert Louis Stevenson
illustrated by David Mackintosh

The Castle of Inside Out, by David Henry Wilson
illustrated by Chris Riddell

Belle and Sébastien, by Cécile Aubry
illustrated by Helen Stephens

The Bears' Famous Invasion of Sicily, by Dino Buzzati
illustrated by the Author

The Wizard of Oz, by L. Frank Baum
illustrated by Ella Okstad

Lassie Come-Home, by Eric Knight
illustrated by Gary Blythe

The Adventures of Pipì the Pink Monkey, by Collodi
illustrated by Axel Scheffler

Just So Stories, by Rudyard Kipling
illustrated by the Author

The Jungle Books, by Rudyard Kipling
illustrated by Ian Beck

Five Children and It, by E. Nesbit
illustrated by Ella Okstad

How to Get Rid of a Vampire, J.M. Erre
illustrated by Clémence Lallemand

Anne of Green Gables, by L.M. Montgomery
illustrated by Susan Hellard

Pollyanna, by Eleanor H. Porter
illustrated by Kate Hindley

Little Women, by Louisa May Alcott
illustrated by Ella Bailey

Black Beauty, by Anna Sewell
illustrated by Paul Howard

Alistair Grim's Odditorium, by Gregory Funaro
illustrated by Chris Mould

Alistair Grim's Odd Aquaticum, by Gregory Funaro
illustrated by Adam Stower

The Secret Garden, by Frances Hodgson Burnett
illustrated by Peter Bailey

Alice's Adventures in Wonderland, by Lewis Carroll
illustrated by John Tenniel

Little Lord Fauntleroy, by Frances Hodgson Burnett
illustrated by Peter Bailey

The Railway Children, by E. Nesbit
illustrated by Peter Bailey

The Wind in the Willows, by Kenneth Grahame
illustrated by Tor Freeman

What Katy Did, by Susan Coolidge
illustrated by Susan Hellard

The Adventures of Sherlock Holmes, by Arthur Conan Doyle
illustrated by David Mackintosh

For our complete list, please visit:
www.almajunior.com